Wind Dancer's Flute

by

Francis Eugene Wood

2010

Published by Tip-of-the-Moon Publishing Co.
Farmville, VA
Printed by Farmville Printing
Photograph by Camden Wood
Book design by F.E.W.
All rights reserved
First U.S. Printing
Email address: fewwords@moonstar.com
web site (http://tipofthemoon.com)

ISBN 0-9657047-2-6

For the children among us
For the child within us

– FOREWORD –

There is a place in the Great Smoky Mountains that I know better than I should. I never lived there, although it is near where my mother was born and reared. It is in the vicinity of a bustling town, and yet, there are no tourists who know of its existence.

That I should know this place nestled within a fold of the forested mountains is a puzzlement to me. That I should know what occurred there is even more mystifying. But I do not question things learned by the soul, and never do I shun the voices of the good spirits who enter my solitude like fairies in a child's dream.

I have this story from long ago. It started with the wind, or should I say the breath of the Great Spirit. Perhaps it was, indeed . . .

Slowly it began, barely as a breath among
the clouds, until it strengthened and came into
the trees, coaxing crisp brown leaves to dance. A
hunter in the sleepy winter forest cocked his head
and listened to what he imagined was a multi-
tude of approaching game. He thought at first it
might be a herd of deer. Then as the sound surrounded him, he thought it could be a great gang
of turkeys come to roost. But no creature showed
hair or feather, and the hunter settled back
against his tree and laid down his gun. The real-
ization that what had caused his moment of
excitement was only the wind brought a smile to
his lips. As dusk encroached upon his place in

the woods, he turned his face to the treetops and watched as they bent playfully towards the west.

On went the wind, and the trees bowed gracefully to its touch. The hemlocks and the pines that cloaked the mountainsides moaned and whistled long, sacred notes as old as time. Skeletal hardwoods held strong, yet rattled their naked upper branches like swordsmen at play. Furry animals huddled warmly in their swaying nests, and the owl ceased to stir.

On went the wind, up and between the rolling hills and down into the valleys and the hollows where it licked the spray from falling streams. Dried, curly leaves lost their holds and swirled from above, launching like vessels onto the surface of frigid rivulets. Through the village swept the wind and beyond, to the dimly lit cabin where would lie its destination.

The expression on Cloud Dancer's face was that of great pain, but the young Cherokee woman would not cry out.

"It will come soon," assured the midwife

who stood at the side of her bed, patting the wet cheeks of the young woman with a cool, dampened cloth. "Soon you will see the face of your child." But she knew something was wrong, for she had been present at many births and could read nature.

Sarah Ogle had been summoned to the cabin of Farley McKeenan by a distant neighbor who had seen Farley's bear-mauled remains laid to rest by a stranger and a priest over in Banner's Hollow three days prior. Knowing that Farley McKeenan had an Indian woman ripe with child, the neighbor had paid a visit and found the young woman in a troubled way.

By the time Sarah Ogle arrived, Cloud Dancer's time was at hand. Sarah could only pray to deliver the child and bring the mother's loss of blood under control.

She placed a couple of oak logs on the fire and stirred a broth she had simmering in a kettle, then washed her hands and wiped them dry on her apron.

The young woman called to her softly.

Sarah leaned over her. "Yes, dear," she said. "I am here with you." She held the cold hands of the young Indian woman in her own and listened.

Cloud Dancer looked into the eyes of the

5

midwife and then past her to the shuttered window across the room. "Open the window so that this child will feel the wind," she said.

Sarah was puzzled. "But it is cold outside, dear," she quietly protested.

Cloud Dancer smiled weakly, then swallowed and said, "The Spirit has spoken to me, and I will live only to give birth to this child." She paused and put her hand to her heart and winced with pain. "Please open the shutters, Miss Sarah," she pleaded.

Sarah Ogle had seen a lot in her day, and she was as strong-willed as any man or woman could be; yet when she heard the plea of that dying woman, she wasted not a second more and was in the midst of pulling open the wooden shutters when Cloud Dancer made her final effort to bring forth her child. Sarah left the shutters half open and barely had enough time to guide the newborn onto the bed before she noticed that its mother had died. The grief-stricken midwife worked quickly to do what was necessary, but when the child did not respond to any of her coaxing, her shoulders slumped and she turned away in tears. "No, God, not both of them," she cried. When she looked down and saw their peacefulness, she placed the tiny boy child in the arms of his mother and sat at the foot of the bed and wept.

Sarah Ogle didn't know what to do. This had never before happened in all her years of midwifery. So she sat there in a tearful daze. She didn't notice the blaze of the fire on the hearth, nor did she hear the forest around the cabin when it began to move. But when the wooden shutters which had been left ajar were forced open by a gust of cold wind, she rose suddenly. And when the still baby lying in the arms of his lost mother gasped for his first breath of life, she rushed to his aid. Astonished, she took the baby in her arms and held it to her bosom, crying softly her thanks to God.

"I will name you Wind Dancer," she said as she gently wrapped him in a warm blanket, "for it was the wind that brought you life."

The next day, Cloud Dancer was laid to rest beside her husband over in Banner's Hollow, and Sarah Ogle crossed over three mountains to her cabin situated on a bluff high above the village that would become a town.

Years passed and Wind Dancer grew to be a handsome young man. He was strong and wise

and possessed a free and pure spirit. Sarah Ogle, whom he called "Singing Bird," loved him as a son and taught him the things he would need to know to live among men. He learned to read so that he would not be lost in the world outside of his own and to understand numbers so that he could not be fooled.

As a young boy, Wind Dancer would accompany Singing Bird when she was called to sit with those in labor, so the folks in the hollows and on the ridges came to know him. He played with their children and was always bringing them treasures from the forest, like smooth stones he collected from the streams or bird feathers.

The one thing Wind was known for most of all was his flute. It was not a new or a very fine flute, and by the time Sarah got it for him, it had more than a few chips and cracks. But Wind took to it as naturally as breathing. And when he would play his music, he would kick up his heels and dance and throw back his head, eyes closed. Yes, Sarah Ogle had taught her adopted son to read and to count, to pray and to be polite among men. But when she heard him play his flute and watched him dance around the trees and wild-flowers, she knew in her heart that he was blessed in a special way.

One day as Wind lay on his side contemplating the procession of a line of small black ants, Sarah approached him.

"Where does your music come from, Wind?" she asked.

The young man sat up and hugged his knees as he looked upon the face of the only mother he had ever known. He smiled and motioned for her to sit on a log beside him. She did so, and then Wind began to speak. "I listened as a baby in your arms, my sweet Singing Bird, when you sang to me in the stillness of the night or when the heavens rumbled and clouds covered the sun and frightened me. I listened to the music of the hoe-downs and the echo of the good folks singing in the hollows on Sunday." He pointed towards the west and said, "Three mountains away lies the village of my blood mother's people. I listen to their songs and wonder at the spirits that move them."

Sarah was not surprised to hear of his visits to the Indian village, for she knew well his interest in the people there. And so she listened as Wind continued.

"I've something to tell you that I have not spoken of before."

"What is it, Wind?" she asked.

Wind smiled, then looked beyond the woman into the surrounding forest. A distant look came over him.

Sarah had seen that look before. "Do you hear something, Wind?"

Wind came out of his reverie and answered softly as if he were sharing a secret. "I always hear things, Singing Bird."

"Oh!" responded the woman as she placed a strand of his long black hair behind his ear. "What is it that you always hear?"

"I hear the butterflies when they flutter about the flowers in the meadow, or there in the garden," he pointed. "I hear the drone of the honey bees, and I count the wing beats of the birds that flit in and out of the tree branches. And when a leaf loses its hold and drifts to the ground, I can hear it, Singing Bird, and not just when it strikes limbs and other leaves, but when it is in the air!" Wind was silent for a moment before he continued. "There is a sound for everything I know in nature. Many of these sounds are like musical notes, and when they blend, it is like the orchestra that you told me you heard when you were a little girl."

"Yes, I remember telling you about that," Sarah recalled. "But I'm surprised you remember. You were so young."

"I remember," replied the young man, smiling. "I cannot sound like an orchestra with

11

my flute, but I can play the solos of nature."
Wind shrugged his shoulders. "And that is where
my music comes from."

The woman frowned. "I am not so lucky,
Wind. To me the buzz from a bee is only a buzz,
and I could not hope to count the wing beats of a
bird!" She held his face in her hands and shook
him playfully, then added, "If what you play on
that flute of yours is what you hear in these hills,
then God bless you, son! That's a gift for sure."

"I reckon you're right, Singing Bird," Wind
agreed. He lifted the flute from the breast pocket
of his coat and began to play.

In the village that would become a town,
things were changing. Where there used to be
one store, now there were two. The dirt footpaths
that used to link one place to another had become
boarded sidewalks that creaked under the weight
of businessmen and other folks moving about.
There were now three churches on the outskirts
of the village and two grain mills alongside the
river. And on any given day of the week except
Sunday there was a bustle about the village that
wasn't there in the past.

So, when Wind walked into the village one Saturday morning after a hard spring rain, he stood in the middle of the street and marveled at all the activity around him--that is, until a horse-drawn buckboard almost ran over him.

"Git out de way, boy!" shouted the driver, as he swerved past the startled young man. The rims of his wagon wheels drove deep into the muddy ruts in the road, sloshing brown, bubbly muck across Wind's knees. He jumped back and was sideswiped by a large horse with a fat rider who pushed at him with a stirruped boot. "Watch out, boy," the man yelled as he hurried by, "or ye goin' te git kilt!"

Wind swung around and made his way to the boardwalk. He stood there for a long time and watched as people went about their business. Loud, well-dressed men stepped in and out of doorways or stood talking in groups. Women pulled their children along, daring their little boys to get mud on their clean britches. There were so many people that Wind couldn't imagine where they had all come from. He wasn't used to crowds, as he had lived most of his life among the people of the ridges and hollows. These people seldom found it necessary to come down into the village. There was no need because Erastus Huskey took orders and made deliveries with his horse-drawn wagon once a season. Wind had never even been to school with other children. Sarah Ogle had taught him to read and write and work with numbers.

Wind was thinking about these things when he heard a voice behind him say, "Hello." The voice was soft and clear, and when he turned around, he saw that it belonged to a girl with golden hair and azure eyes. She stood there in boys' clothes and muddy boots that came up to her knees. Her oversized plaid jacket was unbuttoned, and a light blue scarf hung around her neck. She smiled and said, "My name is Joy. What's yours?"

"Wind," he answered. "My name is Wind Dancer."

Joy looked closely at the young man standing before her. He was perhaps six feet tall and well-proportioned, with broad shoulders and narrow hips. He was square-jawed and quite handsome. She immediately felt drawn to him. His dark eyes seemed to dance, and although he was obviously a bit unnerved, there was a gentleness about him. His manner of dress was somewhat unusual in that it was a blend of styles. He wore a dark morning coat which fit rather loosely and showed its wear around the collar and cuffs. Beneath this was a gentleman's black vest over a white linen shirt. His trousers were of thin gray wool. In contrast, he wore knee-high moccasins which added an untamed elegance to his attire. His black hair flowed freely over the collar of his coat. Two long thin braids touched his lapels.

Joy had never met a person quite like Wind Dancer. "Do you live here?" she asked.

Wind pointed in the direction of his cabin. "I live in the hills, there," he replied.

Joy shuffled her feet and studied the young man's features. "I think that you are of Cherokee descent. Am I right?"

Wind squinted his eyes at the mid-morning sun which shone bright upon the hair of the girl. He could see that she was very lovely, although a bit forward. He decided that he liked her. "My mother was Cherokee and my father Irish."

The girl nodded. "Then I am right. And I am pleased to make the acquaintance of one of the Cherokee people." She reached out her hand and Wind reciprocated. But they did not shake hands. They merely touched for a moment; and in that instant, their hearts danced.

"Ani`-yun`uiya," replied the young man.

The girl questioned him with her eyes.

Wind smiled and said, "It is Cherokee for the Principle People." He motioned for the girl to follow him, and they sat on a crate at the corner of a shop. "Do you know the story of the Cherokee people, Joy?" he asked.

The girl shook her head. "Not really. Only that the ones around here refused to be forced away."

Wind nodded. "The people of my mother would not leave because they lived in the center of the world. You see, the homeland of the Principle People was a floating island of solid rock, held by four cords from the sky. There was a time when everyone lived above the sky, but it was very crowded. So the water beetle went down to explore the sea and found no land. He dived below the water and came up with mud, and that grew until it formed the island of the Earth. When the island was dry enough, the plants and animals came down from the sky. The purpose of the Principle People is to keep their world in harmony and balance."

Joy shook her head. "But the world is so out of sorts, Wind. What happened?"

Wind ran his fingers through his long black hair. "For the answer to that, you need only look around you. There were other worlds the Cherokee knew nothing of, and when those became crowded, they spilled onto the island. That is when the imbalance began."

"Do you think the balance will ever

return?" the girl asked.

Wind drew a long breath and answered, "Only when the tribes of the Earth are small again and live within the center of their own worlds. That is what I think, Joy."

The girl looked intently at her new friend. "Where are your parents?"

"They are dead," he answered. "I live with the only mother I have ever known. Her name is Sarah Ogle, but I call her Singing Bird because she sings so sweetly."

Joy smiled. "I have heard of Sarah Ogle. She is a midwife in the mountains."

Wind nodded. "She has brought many lives into the world."

"Did she tell you about your people?"

"She has told me some things, but most of what I know comes from my mother's brother. His name is Running Wolf, and he visits me sometimes."

Several young children came out of a near-by shop and began skipping about and laughing, until they noticed Wind sitting on the crate. When they approached him, he reached into his coat pocket and brought out his wooden flute. He smiled at the children, then began to play the instrument. Joy had never heard such music in her life, and the children seemed entranced. One girl began to clap her hands and shuffle her feet. It was not long before the other children joined in, and their dancing caught the attention of others. Wind rose from his seat and began a dance of his own. He shuffled his feet on the low notes and kicked up his heels on the high ones. His coat flapped with his movements, and his hair flew wildly about his head and shoulders. Some of the children imitated his movements. A dark-skinned girl with hazel eyes jumped upon the crate and stepped to the music, while a crippled boy sat with his feet in the muck and kept time on the boardwalk with his walking stick.

Joy watched as the children danced and was so moved by the music that soon she, too, was prancing and slinging her long yellow hair in the sunlight. Shoppers and storekeepers wandered out onto the boardwalk to see the goings-on. Some of them tapped their feet and smiled. But there were others who frowned and shook their heads. They grumbled among themselves and pointed.

Wind played and danced and coaxed the children to let themselves go. One tune fed into another, and a frenzy of good-natured abandonment prevailed, until it was broken by the loud thud of a stick against a water trough and the boom of a man's voice shouting, "Stop it!"

18

Some of the children cowered. Others ran looking for their mothers. The crippled boy trembled, and the dark-skinned girl jumped off the crate, into the arms of Joy.

"Stop this nonsense, right now!" shouted the fat man, whose boots were high and muddy and who was wearing a big hat and a long coat. A tin button popped off his bulging vest as he stepped into the middle of the crowd. His eyes were as cruel as his down-turned mouth. His bushy, unkempt eyebrows matched the gray, wiry mustache and beard on his bloated red face.

The weathered boards creaked under his weight as he walked over to Wind. He scowled at the young man and demanded, "Who are ye, boy?"

Wind looked directly into the eyes of the towering man and answered softly, "I am Wind Dancer."

The man snarled. "Well now, Wind Dancer, where might yer folks be?" The man reeked of whiskey.

"My mother and father are dead. I live with my adopted mother, Sarah Ogle."

The man shrugged. "I ain't never heard of no Sarah Ogle," he spat. "How 'bout any o' ye'ns?" He surveyed the faces in the crowd. Eyes looked downward and away, even though most of them knew Sarah and the boy she had adopted. "Well?" shouted the big man.

Finally a frail old man called out, "She's a wid'r up in the moutains 'round here, a midwife. Took 'at young'n on when his Injun ma died. His pa got et up by a bar 'round Banner's Holler, they say."

A woman spoke up. "Sarah's a good woman, and that boy ain't never hurt nobody."

"That's enough," drawled the big man. He turned back to Wind and looked upon him with disgust. He tapped the end of his cane on the boardwalk, then brought it up and poked at the thin braids of hair hanging over the lapels of Wind's coat.

Wind did not break contact with the man's eyes.

"The name's William B. Newton, boy. And I don't want no Injun walkin' or talkin' or playin' no flute 'round here. I don't care if yer ma and pa is livin' or dead, and it don't matter none to me who keeps ye."

Joy, who was stunned by the cruelty of Newton, moved forward to intercede, but a woman took her by the arm and cautioned her, "Ye best stay clear o' him, girl."

"Git on off the boardwalk, boy," demanded Newton. He pushed hard at the chest of Wind, and the young man lost his footing and fell backwards. The flute flew out of his hand and onto the boardwalk. As he reached for it, a muddy boot came down hard on it and crushed it. Then a knee came down hard on the middle of his back.

Joy broke away from the grasp of the woman and struck Newton on the shoulder with her fist. "Get off of him!" she shouted, but one backhand swipe from the enraged man sent her sprawling into the crowd. He pulled a knife and laid his weight upon the back of Wind, pinning him to the boardwalk. There were gasps from the onlookers. Women began pulling their children away from the scene. In an instant, Newton rose with a cruel grin on his face and two long braids of hair in his hand.

Wind tried to get to his feet, but was quickly kicked off the boardwalk and into the muddy street by Newton, who laughed and turned to the crowd. "Everybody knows a Injun likes to stay close to the earth!" he roared. He looked back at Wind and said sternly, "Don't come 'round here no more, Injun, or I'll take more'n yer har." He kicked the splintered flute into the mud and told the crowd to "git on."

The crowd dispersed. Only three people stepped into the street to help Wind Dancer. They were Joy, Emily, the dark-skinned girl, and the

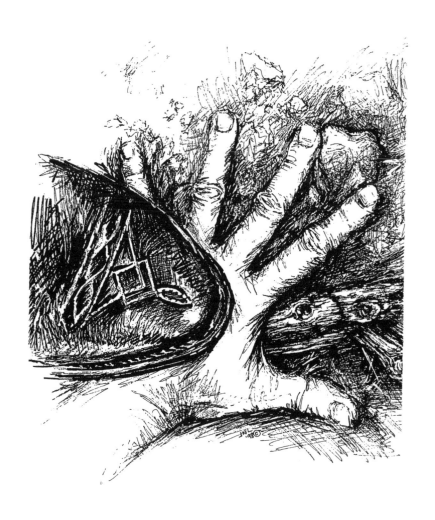

crippled boy named Rag. Joy and Emily helped Wind to his feet and straightened his coat.

Wind could not believe what had happened to him. He could not imagine that a whole village would stand by and let one man force his hatred upon another. But it was done, and the hurt and humiliation burned into his heart. As Rag handed him the splintered flute Sarah Ogle had given him, tears welled in Wind Dancer's eyes.

"He thinks that just because he owns half of this village he owns people, too, Wind." Joy's voice was filled with anger. "Don't let it ruin you, though, 'cause one day he'll get what's coming to him." She brushed the mud off his coat and grasped his arm. "Come on, now. The three of us are going to walk out of here with you."

And so they did. Wind and Joy, Emily and Rag walked up the muddy street and out of the village that would become a town. And as they passed, the people on the boardwalk and in the shops watched with shame in their hearts.

When Sarah Ogle heard about what had

happened to Wind, she was heartbroken. She had always known that he was different and had praised him all of his life for his uniqueness, but now she could not reach him. He was still kind and loving towards her, but a change had come. He had felt the sting of the world, and all of the beauty and goodness he had known was harnessed by the pang of rejection. Sarah worried that his hurt might grow into hatred; so on a warm day while Wind was away in the forest with his friends, she sent word by a trader for his uncle to come.

A week later, Running Wolf appeared at her doorstep. "How is the keeper of my nephew?" he asked as Sarah led him into the cabin.

"I am fine, my old friend," she answered. "But Wind has suffered a bad encounter with someone in the village, and I am afraid for him. No longer does he laugh or tell me his funny dreams or speak of his whimsical ideas. But worst of all, he does not play his music anymore." She told Running Wolf all about what had happened in the village.

He understood well. "Sarah," he spoke, "it is wise that you have summoned me. Wind is at the beginning of his manhood. You will see changes in him. That is normal. There will be things that he will not speak of, things kept inside. But the music must not be kept inside, not with Wind. It is the expression of his soul, the voice of his spirit. Just as Wonkan Tonka, the Great Spirit, blew life into his lungs, so must he continue to express his thanks through that which lightens the hearts of men. It is his gift, and it is more powerful than he knows." Running Wolf touched the hand of his friend. "I will take him into the forest, Sarah, to a place he must go."

Sarah agreed, for she knew that Running Wolf was a wise man.

In the weeks since they had met, Wind and Joy had bonded in their hearts. He, the mixed-blood child of parents he had never known, had been raised by the goodhearted Sarah Ogle who loved and treated him as her own. And Joy, orphaned at the age of eight, had come to live with a widowed great-aunt in the village, where she cared for the elderly woman and managed her affairs. It had been a good arrangement for Joy, as she was afforded much freedom and the opportunity to be herself. It was that same freedom she shared with Wind Dancer. They were possessed of an unbridled spirit, which is always the envy of those held by the tightly cinched noose of society. Wind and Joy were oblivious to all of this. To them the bloom of friendship and the blossom of love had been such a natural progression that those around them became aware of it before they did. Of course, there was some whispering among the village gossips, but as usual with such people, their rumors were conceived of ignorance and squelched desires.

One evening, as the moon rose above the mountain peaks, Rag and Emily said their goodbyes early and headed off towards the village, leaving Wind and Joy alone at their favorite place overlooking a deep hollow. The sound of water far below them became louder as the night grew still.

"What are you thinking of, Wind?" asked the girl as she studied the profile of his face. She knew something was troubling him.

For a while the young man did not answer. Joy laid her head against his shoulder and snuggled against the warmth of his body. She knew that there were answers in silence. She did not repeat her question.

The moon climbed into the sky, and twinkling stars appeared in the darkness. Finally, Wind turned to Joy and lifted her face to his. In the moonlight his eyes were like dark wells, and she felt herself being drawn into them willingly. He swept a strand of hair from her face and kissed her tenderly on the lips.

"I must go away for a few days, Joy," he whispered. "My uncle has spoken to Singing Bird and wants me to go on a journey with him."

Joy pressed her forehead to his neck. "When will you return?" she asked, her voice soft and trembling.

Wind looked at the face of the girl with azure eyes. He saw the twinkle of a star in a tear that lay on her cheek. He kissed it away and smiled. "I will be back soon. Listen to Singing Bird. She always seems to know when folks are coming and going."

Joy smiled and kissed his cheek. "I'll visit her every day," she promised.

"There is something else, Joy." Wind pulled away and stood. He looked up at the moon and stars as if trying to find the right words.

Joy remained sitting. "What is it?"

Wind turned around and faced her. "Would you live here in the mountains with me someday and have my children?" he asked softly. "Would you plant a garden at my side and live off the land? Would you sit beneath the moon and the stars with me forever and speak or be

silent? And if I can play my music again someday, would you dance with me and sing?"

Joy reached out her hands, and Wind
pulled her up to him. They embraced as if they
could not bear to part. "I'll wait for you, Wind
Dancer. And I will be your wife someday," she
assured him.

The day before Wind Dancer was to begin
his journey with Running Wolf, he and Rag
walked along a narrow trail that led to Singing
Bird's cabin.

"Do you think you might one day go back
into the village, Wind?" asked the boy.

"I'm not sure, Rag." He tousled the boy's
hair. "How about you?"

The boy slapped the smooth bark of a
maple tree and answered, "There ain't nothin' fer
me down there, but I ain't scared none. I been
teased and hawked at ever since I was little, but it
didn't git me, 'cause I know somethin'."

"What is it, Rag?" Wind stopped and
looked at his friend. The boy was bent over like
an old man. He had a turned foot, and one leg
was shorter than the other. He was breathing

hard because it took twice the effort just for him to move. But Rag was feisty, and he never gave up at anything.

"I know that no man is better than another. Jest luckier. I ain't never seen one what could take his riches with him when he goes on. So, that puts us all in the same boat. It ain't 'bout what ye got or what yer wearin'. It's 'bout what's inside ye. That's all we take with us."

Wind smiled and patted his friend on the shoulder. "We had better get to the cabin or Singing Bird will worry herself sick." He resumed the lead, and Rag lumbered along behind him.

The forest was an open book to Running Wolf; and although its secrets had been passed on to him by his uncle, he delighted in the smallest of nature's revelations.

And so it was that he led Wind Dancer far away from his home to a place unknown to the young man, a place unruined by man's greed and ownership. A mysterious place that would go unnoticed on a map, for it was on the way to nowhere, and within a stone's throw of nothing desired by man. Yet it was beautiful and ancient, with giant trees and a sparkling stream that rippled with trout. The forest floor was clear of debris, and game was plentiful.

Wind did not know how many days they had walked to get to this place, since he remembered nothing past his third night's rest. So, as he sat in a clearing beneath the sweeping branches of great evergreens, he asked his uncle, "Where are we, Running Wolf?"

The older man smoked his pipe, then answered, "We are in a place known only by a few of the Principle People. It is where things remain as they were in the beginning."

"How did we get here?"

"The pathway is but a scant trace, and few are those who find it."

"But how did we find it?"

Running Wolf answered without hesitation, "By not looking, and following our hearts."

Wind knew he was in a special place, so he waited, hoping his purpose here would be revealed.

After a long silence, Running Wolf spoke. "When the animals and plants came down from the sky, they were tired and tried to stay awake; but only a few did. The panthers and the owls and a few others stayed awake for seven days.

They were given the power to see in the dark. The trees you see about you stayed awake also, and that is why they are green even when most others lose their leaves and sleep in the winter.

"And there were spirits that came into the bodies of little people. They are magic and move from this place into the next and back again."

Wind knew of the little people. All of the Cherokee knew of them. "The little ones?" he questioned.

Running Wolf nodded his head and passed his pipe into the hands of his nephew. "Yes, Yunwi Tsunsdi', the little spirits, dwell here, behind the trees and under the rocks."

Wind looked into the growing darkness. "Do they hear and watch us now, Uncle?"

Running Wolf's face gave the hint of a smile. "Yes, they are here now," he nodded.

"Did they know we were coming?" asked the young man while handing the pipe back to his uncle.

"They knew," admitted Running Wolf, "from the time we left the home of your adopted mother and began our journey into the western mountains. And when I spoke to you of our fasting along the way, they began to prepare for your coming."

"My coming?"

31

"Yes, Wind, *your* coming. This journey is not for me. I am only your guide, for I have been here before as a boy."

Wind was surprised. "You have a good memory, Uncle, to find the way after so long a time."

The man looked up into the shadows of the trees, then said to his nephew, "Remember, Wind, the trace is scant. On the third day of our walk, while we rested by a stream and you closed your eyes, I was visited by Tsawa'si and Tsaga'si, the little spirits who told me that we should follow them."

Wind was astonished, for he thought that Running Wolf knew the path of their journey all along.

The man continued. "Tsawa'si and Tsaga'si are the little spirits who show the hunter where to find game so that his people will not go hungry. They also help him find his way when he is unsure of his path."

"But if they led us here, why could I not see them?" asked Wind.

"Because, until now, you have only seen with your eyes." Running Wolf arose from his place and turned away from his nephew.

"Where are you going, Uncle?"

"I am tired and shall find a place in the

leaves to make my bed. You remain here, for you are about to see beyond what you know." With that, Running Wolf walked quietly into the surrounding darkness.

Wind Dancer listened until he could no longer hear his uncle. He strained his eyes but could see nothing in the great forest. All was silent except for the trickle of the nearby stream. He thought about the words his uncle had spoken. Then he remembered something Running Wolf had told him when he was a young boy, "Look at the world and men with your eyes; but look into the world and men with your spirit."

Wind Dancer closed his eyes and thought about his life and how wonderful it had been growing up in the cabin of Sarah Ogle. He knew his blood mother could not have loved him more than she. He remembered his music and how it had made his spirit soar. He recalled the faces of the children as they listened to him play, and then he remembered Joy. He could almost smell the sweet fragrance of her skin and see her calming smile, her golden hair, and her eyes like the clearest sky--Joy, the good friend with whom he had fallen so deeply in love.

Then he remembered the stare of hatred and the pain of the humiliation he had suffered. No one in the village had helped him. They had stood there, many of whom had known him all of his life, and had allowed one cruel-hearted man to voice his loathing and wield his power. And in doing so, they had allowed one to speak for them all.

Wind clenched his teeth and shook his head as the hurt and anger arose from deep within him. Then he heard something. At first it was like a dull, distant thud. He opened his eyes and searched into the darkness. "Drums," he whispered. The sound grew louder, and he realized that it was not from any one direction but all around him. Louder it became, until it sounded as if the drummers were upon him. His nerves were taut, and he could feel his heart in his throat! Suddenly the drumming stopped, and through the blackness, he saw a small light. It moved slowly and low to the ground, illuminating the face of its carrier. As it drew nearer, he saw that it was the face of a man, a man much shorter than Wind Dancer's knee. On he came, until he stood opposite Wind. The glow of the coals, which the little man held before him, allowed Wind to examine him in detail.

He was a rather thin, but well-muscled, person, dressed in a skin breechclout which was trimmed in blue cloth. His shoulders were broad for one so small, and around his neck he wore a strand of shining stones which reflected the burning coals. His facial expression was stern yet devoid of malice. His eyes were dark and set close together. His facial features were finely chiseled, and his long black hair fell loosely upon his shoulders and over his chest. The man carried no weapons at his side. His moccasins laced up to his knees.

Wind thought that he looked like a very small Cherokee dressed in the old way. He was about to address the little man, when, all of a sudden, there was movement around him. In the blink of an eye, sticks were laid for a fire, and little hands withdrew into the shadows.

Then the man standing before Wind spoke, "I am Atsil'dihye'gy, the fire carrier."

Wind's nerves began to settle down when he heard the Cherokee language. He watched as the fire carrier laid the coals beneath the neatly arranged sticks and gently blew until a small flame was born.

The little man stood and smiled. "I have brought you light so that you may see my brothers and sisters."

Wind nodded, and the little man backed away and sat upon a log, but as soon as Wind blinked his eyes, the fire carrier was gone. A rustle in the leaves made him turn his head. He looked back towards the fire and saw that three little people stood across from him. These were much smaller than the fire carrier, perhaps the height of a man's hand. The two men were dressed much the same as Atsil'dihye'gy. A woman sat between the men. She was naked except for a skirt of animal hair. Shining bracelets adorned her ankles and wrists, and her feet were bare. Her hair, long and black, with several gray strands, had been braided. It was parted in the middle and covered her breasts.

Wind thought that she was quite beautiful. "Who are you?" he asked.

"I am Diya," the little woman answered, "and this," (she touched the arm of the man to her left) "is Unwa of the Water Dwellers, and here" (she touched the man at her right side) "is Tewyhe of the Rock Dwellers." The woman paused and smiled. "I am of the People Who Live Anywhere," she said proudly.

"Why have you come to see me?" Wind asked.

The three huddled together and spoke in a language unknown to Wind. They parted and Diya spoke, "*You* have come to us, Wind Dancer."

Wind was puzzled. He ran his fingers through his hair and rubbed his chin. There was a snap of a twig behind him in the shadows, and he thought he heard a small snicker. "I do not understand," he admitted.

The three little ones huddled together and conversed among themselves in their secret language, then parted again. Diya came closer to the fire. "We represent the tribes of the Yunwi Tsunsdi', the little people who have known of you since the night Wonkan Tonka breathed life into your body. You are of the Chosen Clan, Wind Dancer, set apart even from the clan of your mother, who entered into the shadowland upon your birth. Being such, your spirit possesses a gift whose power is great. You have only touched the surface of that power. It is your music, the language which transcends all races of people."

Wind was confused. "I never thought of my music as a language," he confided.

"Ah, but it is!" responded the little woman. "And yours is the very source of nature. That is why you hear it in the rain and the wind. Its rhythm is in the flutter of wings and distant thunder. Its movements are of violent storms and warm summer mornings.

"What men hear and take for granted, you breathe into your spirit and compose from your heart. That is why they listen when you play your flute. Children listen because their hearts are pure, their spirits are free. Their mothers and their fathers listen because they long for the innocence of youth." Diya pointed at the flicker of the firelight around them. "Look, Wind Dancer," she said. "See how the light dances among the trees?"

Wind looked around him, and everywhere there was movement.

Diya continued. "The spirits of those who hear your music will also dance. Just like nature, the music is boundless and never ending. It has the power to calm and to heal, and to do things you have never imagined."

The young man questioned the little woman with his eyes.

"If you beckon nature with your music and the cause is pure, then it will respond to your wish." Diya ran around the fire and jumped upon the knee of the young man, then added almost in a whisper, "But there cannot be a doubt as to the outcome, Wind Dancer. You must always be sure of what you desire."

Diya ran down Wind's leg and slid off his moccasin and onto the ground. She resumed her place between Unwa and Tewyhe.

Silence prevailed for a while, until Wind spoke out. "I fear I cannot play the music anymore, Diya. Besides, my flute is ruined."

Diya thought for a moment, then elbowed

Unwa, who cleared his throat and spoke. "You have lost only your innocence, Wind Dancer. You have felt the sting of man's hatred. Will you let his poison consume you, or will you cleanse yourself and walk above it?"

Wind thought for a moment, then answered, "The people who knew me did nothing. They just stood there and--"

Tewyhe raised his hand and interrupted. "Men are weak, Wind Dancer, and allow themselves to be ruled by fools. When they begin to see their own reflections in those fools, that is when they break away. Let not one man's cruelty become every man's sin. Remember this, Wind Dancer."

Wind listened closely to the words of Tewyhe and understood. "I still have no flute," he sighed.

Diya looked into the shadows and waved her hand. Suddenly, a dozen or more little people ran up to the fire and threw sticks on it until its flames reached high and the area was illuminated. It was then that Wind Dancer saw them. Scores of little people appeared from around trees and rocks, even on the branches above him. He was afraid to move for fear that he might squash one beneath his weight. There was much high-pitched chatter among them, and some of

the younger ones began climbing onto his britches and upon his shoulders. Wind chuckled as he helped one fellow who had fallen head first into his coat pocket. Retrieving the kicking little man, he placed him on his shoulder next to two others. "There now," he said, laughing. "A bird's eye view." He looked at the Yunwi Tsunsdi' and could hardly believe that such a race of people really existed.

Things were beginning to get a little unruly, when a shrill yodel gained everyone's attention. Diya stood atop a fallen tree and raised her hands. "Listen, people of the forest! Wind Dancer of the Chosen Clan is without his flute."

There was a fair amount of giggling, and several audible "shushes" before Diya continued. "Can we remedy this situation?" she asked.

The little ones shouted their approval, and a pathway opened amongst them. Wind watched as at least a dozen little men marched up to him, carrying the most beautiful flute he had ever seen.

They laid it on the ground at his feet and stood in silence. Wind reached down and carefully picked up the instrument. Turning it over in his hands, he saw that it was made of hardwood. It was longer than his old flute, and its headpiece was uniquely carved. "An eagle," he marveled as he ran his fingers over the smooth wood. He noticed that long, slender feathers had been etched into its bore so that where one ended another began. These etchings were lightly stained and barely charred so that they resembled real feathers.

Wind brought the flute to his lips and began to play. The tune came from his heart, and its haunting, mystical sound held the little people mesmerized. The purity of the flute's tone and timbre was unlike anything Wind had ever heard. Tears welled in his eyes as he played. When finally he finished, there was silence among the Yunwi Tsunsdi' until Wind laughed and shouted, "Let's dance, little ones!"

There was a roar of approval as an area was cleared for the young man to shuffle his feet. The sound of drums began to echo through the Sacred Forest as Wind Dancer played his flute, and dancing shadows mingled with the trees.

In the shadows a proud man smiled and smoked his pipe. He offered up a prayer to Wonkan Tonka, then watched as his nephew kicked high into the air. "You are almost there, son of my sister," he said softly. "Almost there."

"I seen somethin' mighty perdy today," offered Emily teasingly, as she carefully braided Joy's long strands of golden hair. "An' Miss Sarah told me I ain't seen nothin', but I surely did!" The girl giggled as she peeked around at the face of her friend.

Joy looked out over the mountains and feigned indifference until she could no longer contain herself. Her attempt to veil her excitement was successful only because she looked away as she spoke. "Emily, you are without a doubt a busybody and a tattletale," she scolded with a grin.

"Well," replied the girl, "I jest said I seen somethin', that's all." She finished her braiding and sat down next to Joy. "An' I think Wind Dancer's gonna like it more'n you."

"Oh, he will?"

Emily picked up the little vine and twig basket she had been working on earlier and looked closely at her craftsmanship. "You know what, Joy?" she asked.

"I know you, Emily, and you are dying for me to ask you about that old dress Miss Sarah's making for me." She waited a few seconds, then stated flatly, "Well, I'm not going to ask you a thing."

Joy rested her chin on one knee and looked

at the setting sun. It was beautiful. She wondered if Wind Dancer was watching it at that moment. The thought somehow made her feel closer to him. They had watched so many sunsets together since they had met. They would sit on the rock outcrop and talk. That is what Joy loved most about Wind. He would tell her stories of the forest and its people. He knew so many legends, and he was proud of his heritage and would always speak highly of the Cherokee. Sarah Ogle had told the girl how Wind came to be her son, and Joy knew that he was special. That is why it saddened her that he had lost his will to play his music. He had been so happy and full of life that day in the village. The children had flocked to him. It was all so natural and pure.

A gentle breeze moved up from the hollow, and a rustling in the leaves behind the two girls caught their attention.

It was Rag. "Look what I got," he announced triumphantly, standing there bent over and with a big grin on his face.

Emily stood up and ran over to him. "That's jest what we need, Rag," she said happily. "Them's the perdiest little vines I ever seen."

Rag had cut and pulled wild grape vines into long strands which hung around his arms and shoulders like ropes.

Emily examined them and announced, "Rag, you an' me are goin' to do us up some baskets they'll be scrappin' fer in the village." She smiled and grasped Rag's arm, leaning her head against his strong shoulder. Rag blushed. He didn't say anything, but Joy could tell he loved the attention. It was very obvious that Emily adored the older boy.

"We'd better git on down the mountain, girls," Rag finally announced. "There's a chill in the air, and it'll be dark soon."

Emily ran over and retrieved the little basket she had been working on. "Come on, Joy," she coaxed.

"You two go on. I'll be right behind you as soon as the sun disappears."

Emily looked sadly at Rag, then knelt beside Joy and placed her hand on the shoulder of the girl she admired so much. "He's gonna be jest fine, Joy, an' sooner than you know, the two of you'll be sittin' close right here on this rock." She patted Joy's shoulder and added, "Don't you worry none 'bout that Wind Dancer. He'll be back, 'cause I know somethin'." She nodded her head and cocked an eyebrow.

"What's that?" Joy asked, her eyes filled with tears.

"Wind Dancer loves you, Joy," answered

Emily with a smile. "There ain't no doubt about it either!" Emily touched her friend's cheek, then stood and walked over to Rag.

"Don't you be long, Joy," called Rag as he and Emily started down the trail.

Joy watched them disappear into the forest. She heard Emily giggle a few times, and then all was silent except for the distant rush of wind and water from the hollow. She thought about Emily and Rag and how they were almost inseparable these days. They had been two wonderful, but lonely, people until they found each other. Now they were happy. Emily, the young girl from a poor, fatherless family, had never had more than a ragged hand-me-down dress to wear in all of her life, and yet she was without envy or sadness.

And Rag, the sweet, soft-spoken boy whose body was bent and crippled--she wondered if in his youth he had ever dreamed of running and playing like the other boys in the village. Once he had said to her, "I don't lack nothin', Joy, 'cause I got me a good mama and papa who ain't scared to let me be myself." Joy had a good feeling about Emily and Rag, and there was no doubt in her mind that they belonged together.

Joy sighed and made a frame with her fingers and positioned it so that the descending sun was in its center. She kept it there until it disappeared behind a mountain. The forest was still now, and above her in the northern sky she saw the first star. She remembered a saying her aunt had taught her when she was small. "Are you dressed for bed, child?" the old woman would call from her chair in the den. Joy smiled as she recalled what came next, "Remember, the first star sees you the way you are." The girl had never forgotten that, and often when she walked alone, she wondered how she had been seen from above. She reached out and drew an imaginary circle around the star with her finger. "I'm not alone tonight, star," she said. "I'm by myself, but I'm not alone, not anymore."

She heard the faint call of her name and knew that Rag and Emily would go no farther without her. For a moment she closed her eyes and said a prayer. And then she whispered something soft and sweet, a confession of her heart before a distant light.

After three days in the Sacred Forest, Running Wolf and Wind Dancer departed, the latter having acquainted himself with many new friends.

"We will be your ears and eyes for all time, Wind Dancer," they had said.

"And I will play you a song every day," he had promised.

Never before had Running Wolf seen so great a gathering of the little ones. But Wind Dancer was of the Chosen Clan, and the little people had a special interest in him.

The night before Wind Dancer was to arrive home, he and Running Wolf sat beside a small fire. The older man smoked his pipe while he listened to Wind play his new flute. Sarah Ogle will be pleased, he thought. A girl named Joy would also be pleased, but in a much different way. Running Wolf smiled, for he knew also that the spirit of Wind's mother was pleased. He knew the Yunwi Tsunsdi' did favors for unsuspecting, but worthy, individuals. This, however, was the first time he had ever known them to present such a gift to anyone. They knew the importance of this young man.

Wind played his flute into the night. At times his songs were so happy that it seemed to Running Wolf that the notes skipped between the stars in the sky. And then there were songs of sadness when he imagined Wind grieving for his dead mother and father, or longing for the girl of his heart.

When Wind put down his flute, he spoke. "I have thought much of what the little people said, and I know their words are true."

Running Wolf nodded, but did not speak.

Wind continued. "It is hard, Uncle, to live in a place where one's dignity has been bruised."

Running Wolf was not surprised that Wind said these words, so he replied, "When my mother was young, the blue soldiers came and herded the people together like cattle so that they could move them to the western lands. Treaties had been signed by foolish men who acted with power they did not possess. Promises were made by a government unworthy of trust. The Cherokee were divided, and most were forced away to the edge of their world. The trail is marked by tears and graves. But there were some who stayed by legal means and others who escaped the soldiers. Our mother remained here with her people."

Running Wolf stared into the fire and then looked at his nephew. "You, Wind Dancer, are of the clan of your mother. You are also of the Chosen Clan of the spirits. Will you be moved to the edge of your world by the cruelty of one man and the foolishness of others, or will you remain and face this injustice with a peaceful nature and forgiving heart? That is your decision to make. We are of the Principle People; therefore, it is our responsibility to maintain harmony and balance in the world."

When Running Wolf had finished, he lay down and wrapped himself in his sleeping blanket and closed his eyes. But Wind Dancer remained awake until the fire was nothing more than glowing embers.

Wind's homecoming was a happy one. Sarah Ogle had invited a number of her friends and many of the children of the mountains to a delicious feast.

Joy had met him on the trail to Sarah's cabin. How beautiful she was to him, standing there alone in the golden hues of the late afternoon sun! Her dress was yellow, and even from a distance, he knew there were tiny floral designs on it, for he had seen the material before in Sarah Ogle's sewing basket. The dress was trimmed in white lace at the neck and sleeves, and a white ribbon brought it snug around the girl's slender waist. He smiled when he noticed her bare feet,

but that was Joy. He knew she didn't own a pair of women's shoes. What britches and flannel shirts had hidden from view was now accentuated by the drape of femininity.

Running Wolf had seen the girl from a distance and stepped off the path towards the ridgetop trace to the cabin. He knew the young lovers would have much to talk about. And he was right. But for a long moment they were silent. A squirrel rustled the new foliage in the top of a poplar tree, and a flower broke from its stem. Wind looked up and saw its descent. He rushed forward and caught it in midair. "This is for you," he said, offering it to Joy.

The girl reached out and took the flower. She held it in her palm. Its green, rounded petals and orange base were delicately touched by the fading sunlight. Its fragrance was sweet. "It is lovely," she said as she tucked it into her hair, which was pulled back into a braid. "Thank you, Wind."

Wind stepped closer to the girl. "I have missed you, Joy," he said softly, watching her eyes. He noticed a tear and saw how she touched her heart with one hand and held the other out to him. He took her hand and pulled her to him, and they kissed, tears mingling with laughter. Rustlings in the leaves and wee whispers and chuckles went unnoticed by the two lovers. But all around them were spying little eyes, for now Wind Dancer would always be protected by the Yunwi Tsunsdi'.

Wind and Joy sat upon a rock, and she listened to his every word as he told of his journey and all that had happened. She was happy because the light had returned to his eyes. Finally, she rose and pulled him up by his hands. "You must tell it all to me again, Wind, but now we must hurry. Miss Sarah's been cooking all day."

Wind kissed her again and squeezed her hands. "Then we should hurry," he agreed.

Together they ran along the path towards the cabin of Sarah Ogle.

Wind Dancer played his flute that night, and never had his music sounded sweeter. There was vigor in his dance; and when he leaped high into the air, children laughed and parents gasped. A large fire had been placed in the front yard of the cabin. This was where the mountain folk gathered and feasted and where they watched the young man reveal himself as never before.

When fiddles stopped playing and the crackle of the fire blended with murmuring voices lulling babies to sleep, Wind stood in the firelight and spoke, "I have been on a journey, my friends, and have learned that until now I was a stranger in my own life."

All were attentive around the young man as he looked into their faces. Sarah Ogle felt a lump rise in her throat and the gentle caress of Joy's hand on hers.

Wind continued, "I am Wind Dancer, the son of an Irishman and a Cherokee woman. I am of the clan of my mother. I was born still, until the wind gave me life. I was raised by one who sings like a lark." His eyes fell upon the face of Sarah Ogle. "She is my Singing Bird and my mother. I could not love her more had she borne me. She has given me love and a home and the freedom to be who I am.

My uncle, Running Wolf, the brother of my blood mother, is a shadow in the forest to most of you. But to me he is a teacher who has allowed my mistakes to be my lessons. Just as Singing Bird has taught me the ways of one people, so has he taught me the ways of another." He found the face of his uncle at the edge of the firelight.

"You all know what happened to me in the village, but you must do as I have chosen to do and put it behind you. Do not speak of it again, but pray that there will come a time when hatred will leave the hearts of men. When color and creed or even faith in something is no longer the mark of acceptance or rejection."

The crowd murmured, and Wind saw the little children sitting shoulder-to-shoulder around the fire. Their skins were white and brown and red. They had feasted and danced and laughed together. This night the world was small, but perfect.

"Look at us," he said. "Are we not the blend of nations?" There were nods and words of agreement among the people.

"I will go back into the village," promised the young man. "But I will not shout my words." He held up his flute. "I speak the universal language, but my actions say what is in my heart."

Wind put the flute to his lips and began to play tenderly. He walked around the fire and bent low to fill the ears of the children with the sweetest notes. So distant, yet familiar, was the tune that all of the people, especially the children, knew they had heard it somewhere before. But only Wind Dancer knew from whence it came.

The evening was cool and gentle as Erastus Huskey walked slowly up the winding path through the woods beside Newton's Mill. He could have taken the main road out of the village, but he wasn't in a rush; and he liked the solitude of the little trail. He noticed that the fish were snapping at young mosquitoes in the eddies around the mill, and he wished he could stop to fish. But he had a chore to do, and he passed on by. He reached into his coat pocket and brought out a twist of tobacco. It was dark and moist. He cut sparingly with a worn blade and set the thin plug between cheek and gum. The flavor was sweet. Erastus topped the hill and looked into the treetops. There was not the first hint of a breeze, and yet he was uneasy. Fires made him that way, especially big ones. He studied the lay of the land and the hugh brush piles he was to torch.

There were three of them. Two were near the center of the clearing, and one a little too close to the treeline. He wished William Newton had burned them in early winter when the ground was covered in snow. Then he wouldn't have had to worry about a stray spark. But Newton wouldn't hear of it then--said he was too busy and couldn't get any help. Erastus knew that was a lie. Newton could have had all the help he needed. Up in the hills there were plenty of men who needed work in the winter. But William B. Newton didn't like to part with his money. And he had more of that than he had good sense.

He owned another mill east of the village and three warehouses and most of the shop buildings on the western end. Not bad for a big-mouthed braggart from the East who'd been around for less than a decade. The word was that he'd made his money in shipping, but details were vague.

He was bold as he was big, so he didn't think too long about putting up warehouses and buying into the future of a village that would become a town. He could see it was a bustling place, and the prospects for tourist trade really excited him. He owned one hotel already.

He was on the town council and the bank board and had his fingers into just about every little function going on. Newton was big in the church, too, always sitting on the front pew and singing louder and flatter than any other sinner in the house. Some folks said that Newton was too big, and they weren't talking about his belly either. They were tired of his big mouth and his hand on everybody's back. William B. Newton was big, loud, and rich, but he was not well liked. As a matter of fact, he was loathed by most folks and tolerated by a few. The problem was that he had a mean and greedy nature, and everybody knew it.

Erastus had done a little work for Newton from time to time, but for the most part stayed his distance. He wouldn't have been up on the flat that evening reaching in his pocket for a match, if it wasn't for the fact that his wagon had broken down and he'd missed delivering spring supplies up in the hills. Newton offered him twenty-five dollars to burn off the flat so he could build a new hotel there. Erastus had accepted Newton's offer, all along thinking he'd get help when the time came. It just so happened that on the days following rains when he would rather have burned those brush piles, he couldn't get anyone interested in helping him. Then Newton cornered him one day and threatened to start his own little delivery business if Erastus didn't get that flat burned off "pronto."

Erastus checked the treetops again and looked at the sunset. He wet a flat stone with tobacco spit. Then he struck a match and laid fire to a fatwood stick. He waited until the stick was burning good, then easily stuffed it up under some leaves and debris which he knew would catch fast. He stood back and watched the thick smoke filter through the leaves until they began to burn. The flame grew quickly, as its fuel was dry; and by the time Erastus set the second brush pile on fire, the first one was a roaring inferno. The blaze rose high; and to Erastus' delight, the two middle fires were burning down pretty good when he finally set a flaming fatwood stick to the last brush pile. It caught fast, and in seconds flames were licking the sky.

But Erastus was worried because, when he turned around and faced the west, he felt a cool breeze on his face, a breeze that was not there minutes ago. He walked around the burning brush pile and nervously looked at the timberline next to it. If just one burning leaf drifted into the forest, he knew there would be trouble; so he stood there ready to stomp out any flame that might start. After a while, the fire died down to where he felt more comfortable about it. Then he moved over to the others and tidied them up.

By midnight, Erastus determined his chore to be completed. He walked around the fire closest to the treeline several times and threw burning sticks into it. He then faced the west and decided that the wind had died down sufficiently. By the time he headed down the mill path, the brush piles were nothing more than smoldering embers. He'd collect his pay in the morning, he figured; and while he was at it, he'd get permission from Newton to fish those eddies by the mill. At one o'clock in the morning, Erastus Huskey was snoring peacefully beside his wife at the east end of the village, satisfied that his chore had been finished.

A black bear lumbered along a trace behind the little house on the edge of the village where Joy lay sleeping in her bed. The sound of his passing would have gone unnoticed, except for the fact that the heavy bruin moved along less cautiously than usual and snapped a dry twig. Joy's eyes opened instinctively, and she sat up and looked out the open window. She rubbed her eyes and stared into the moonlit forest. It was gray and black, except for a flicker of light she thought she noticed against the smooth bark of a fat maple tree. Joy blinked and looked again. She had sat and looked out her window and into the darkness before and had never noticed such a flicker. She poked her head out of the bedroom window and peered around to her right. There were more flickers of light against the other trees. Quickly but quietly, she got out of bed and pulled on her clothes. She tiptoed to the front door and opened it. A rush of warm smoke-filled air struck her face as she stepped out of the doorway. She looked to the west and couldn't believe her eyes! The entire mountain between the mill creek and the south ridge was on fire. A strong wind was fanning it furiously down the mountainside towards the village.

Joy rushed in and awakened her aunt, then ran out of the house, shouting "Fire!" and pointing. The fire bell sounded and half-dressed men ran wildly into the streets, heading towards the fire station. William B. Newton came out of his front door and was stunned. Most of his buildings, his warehouses, and one mill were on the west side of the village. If one of those warehouses caught fire, the flames would engulf them all and feed into the village, building by building. A sufficient fireline had never been cut at the western end of the village; thus, there were trees scattered among the warehouses.

Newton ran into the street, shouting and grabbing at men's collars. "My buildings!" he screamed. "Don't let them burn! My mill! Oh, no, the mill!" He ran, gasping, up the street, pushing people out of his way. A water wagon pulled by two wild-eyed horses came out of the firehouse and nearly ran over him, but Newton sidestepped and grabbed on to the wagon, pulling himself up. "Let's git to the mill!" he demanded of the driver.

"Fergit it, Newton," shouted the driver. "Yer mill's 'bout gone! We gotta wet down them warehouses 'fore they go up, or the whole place'll be gone!"

Newton clinched his teeth. "That damn fool Erastus," he growled. "I'll kill him!"

No one heard William B. Newton. He could have shouted at the top of his lungs. It wasn't his buildings anymore or what he could demand of men or offer them. It was survival that was on everyone's mind, and Newton's wealth and prestige had nothing to do with it. William B. Newton was being humbled by nature and his own stupidity.

Joy met Emily and Rag in front of her house. The smoke was so thick it burned their eyes. She pointed towards a large group of women and children who were milling anxiously in the street. "Rag, you and Emily lead those people across the shallow place on Mill Creek," she shouted. "Get them up the hill, out of this smoke. I'm going after Wind."

"You be careful, Joy. That smoke'll get ye 'fore the fire will!" Rag shouted back, as he took Emily by the hand.

Joy ran behind her house and leaped up

the hill onto the game trace. She hurried westward into the smoke, until it became so thick she could hardly see. Then she turned up the ridge through the mountain laurel. Limbs slapped against her body as she crashed and ducked through the thick laurel. Once, she became so entangled that she could hardly move. She looked down into the smoke-filled streets of the village and was terrified. "Wind!" she called. "Oh, God, let me get to him!" She broke free and climbed with all her strength, while to the west the fire roared down the mountainside towards the first of Newton's warehouses.

When Joy topped the ridge, she fell into a steady stride that kept her moving at a good pace towards the cabin of Sarah Ogle. If she could continue, maybe it wouldn't be too late. She knew Wind could do something. If he would do something. If he had in fact forgiven in his heart. But what if he hadn't? What if he said, "They deserve it. Newton deserves it." No, she thought. Wind had spoken from his heart.

Joy was exhausted and could go no farther. She fell to the ground and began to sob. "Oh, God, let me get to him," she cried. But she could not get up. Joy rolled onto her back. That was when she saw tiny silhouettes on the tree limbs above her. She wiped her eyes with bruised hands and looked again, this time more closely. The moon was full, and along the branches of the trees there were wee, dark, human figures. "Little ones," she called, "help me!"

There were small whispers, and then the leaves around her began to rustle. She sat up and, in the moonlight, found herself surrounded by little people.

"It is all right, child," came a small voice.

"Wind told me about you," the girl said. "I need to get to him to tell him that--"

The little voice interrupted. "Go back to the village. We have told Wind Dancer, and he is on his way."

"Oh, thank you, little ones!" Joy cried, wiping her face with her sleeve. But when she looked around, they had disappeared. "Little ones!" she called. There was no answer. She turned and headed back towards the village.

The Yunwi Tsunsdi' had come to Wind Dancer with news of the fire. They awakened him with urgent calls only he would know and spoke to him from his window. "The forest is burning, and the village is threatened," they had said. "Joy beckons you."

Without hesitation, Wind flew from his bed and left the cabin of Sarah Ogle. He ran through the forest with the swiftness of a deer. As he neared the village, it looked as if the heavens were ablaze. "Tell her I'm coming, my friends," he called into the forest as he ran. "Tell her Wind Dancer comes!"

Flames rushed down the western slope, consuming dead and dried debris left by the ravages of winter snow and ice. Men fought furiously, but were unable to prevent the flames from engulfing the first of Newton's warehouses. It fell before his red, watery eyes, and he sank to his knees as fire climbed up the west end of the second one. All is lost, he thought. All of his buildings would go up in flames in this one night.

A man shouted to him, "Come on, Newton. Ain't nothin' to do now but go back to the shops and try waterin' em down!"

Two men pulled the big man onto his feet, and a great gust of wind brought hot smoke and flames hurtling towards them. "Let's git outta here!" they shouted. Then everyone ran back to the stores. The water wagon was rolled into position and bucket lines were formed. Everywhere men and women worked to save their village. But not William B. Newton. He was spent, and he sat down on the boardwalk in a daze.

"We can't stop it!" cried a woman.

"Keep on trying!" shouted someone else.

Erastus Huskey was in the bucket line closest to Newton.

"You!" the big man shouted. "I'm gonna--"

Before he could finish his threat, the second of his three warehouses collapsed, sending a thick cloud of choking smoke towards the people. Some of them threw down their buckets and ran, while others fell to the ground, coughing.

As the smoke cleared, Erastus saw the figure of a man standing alone and facing the sweeping flames. "Look!" he shouted, pointing. The man was only a silhouette against the flames. Even so, Erastus knew who it was.

"Wind Dancer!" called a voice. It was Joy.

Erastus and Newton looked behind them and saw the girl running toward them. "What the--" started the big man.

"Quiet, Newton," she said, stopping directly in front of him.

He snarled at the girl. "What's he doing here?"

"You couldn't begin to understand," she

answered.

Newton was at his wit's end. Fire was about to take hold of his last warehouse. He raised his hand to strike the girl out of his way. And he would have, too, but for the grasp of a strong hand around his wrist. The power was such that it brought him to his knees. He looked up to see the face of an Indian.

"Be quiet and remain still," said Running Wolf in a low voice, as he released his grip on Newton. He put out a hand to Joy and drew her close to him.

As flames swept towards the roof of the warehouse and curled beneath its eaves, Wind Dancer brought his flute to his lips and closed his eyes. He said a prayer, and then began to play.

The people of the village could hardly believe that he could stand so close to the fire. They couldn't imagine what he was doing. But when they heard the faint sound of his flute above the roar of the fire, they felt something was about to happen.

They noticed that the wind calmed. No longer were the flames being coaxed. Wind

Dancer played louder and, with one hand, reached towards the heavens. Immediately, there was a flash of lightning, followed by a clap of thunder so intense that it shook the ground. Joy felt the first drops of rain. She looked at Running Wolf and noticed a smile had formed on his face. He nodded his head and pulled her closer to him.

People stood in awe as rain began to fall in sheets. Wind Dancer moved his feet, first very slowly, and then more rapidly. As he danced, the wind returned at gale force. It blew the torrential downpour into every burning ember until the fire was quenched and only smoke remained.

The wind ceased when the dance ended. The rain stopped when the flute fell silent. And when it was all done, Wind Dancer turned and walked towards Joy and Running Wolf.

Joy met him halfway and flung her arms around his neck. "I knew you would come, Wind," she cried softly.

"Are you all right?" he asked while holding her in his arms.

Joy looked into his eyes and smiled. "I am now," she answered. "We all are now."

Quiet words of their hearts were spoken, and then, together, they approached Newton, who sat in the mud, seemingly stunned by what had just occurred.

Wind reached down and pulled the big man to his feet. "I hope there is something left for you," he said to the man who had humiliated him.

Newton opened his mouth as if to speak, but the words would not come. He lowered his eyes in confusion and shame.

Running Wolf placed a hand on Wind's shoulder. "I am proud of you, Wind Dancer, for on this night you have become a man."

Erastus Huskey patted Wind on the back. "Thank ye, Wind," he said. "Ye kin play fer my pardy any time." Then the frail little man looked at William B. Newton, standing there wet, muddy, and red-faced, and said, "I told ye it were too dry to burn brush, Mr. Newton."

Newton didn't say a word. He just turned and trudged off towards his house.

The sun was rising when Rag and Emily found Wind and Joy.

"Boy, that was some rain come outta nowhere," Rag said, shaking his head. "I couldn't believe it."

"Well, I believe it!" Emily pulled at her damp clothes. "I'm wet to the bone."

Joy squeezed Wind's hand and winked at him. "I believe it, too, Emily," she said. "It was right out of nowhere."

Epilogue

Wind Dancer and Joy were married and lived in the cabin of Sarah Ogle until her death. At that time, they moved three mountains away into a larger cabin that Wind re-built. Here, in the place of his birth, they raised a big family and lived a long and happy life.

Their descendants, scattered throughout the Great Smoky Mountains, tell that upon his death, Joy returned Wind Dancer's flute to the Yunwi Tsunsdi' in the Sacred Forest.

A Note From The Author

This story began as a narrative around one of many wilderness campfires shared with one who has traveled with me for many years. I am grateful to my cousin, Ben Johnson, for always being a willing, if not "captured" audience for my endless imaginings and fireside renderings.

It is my hope that you will enjoy this story and discover some of the rich history which surrounds the Cherokee people. While much of the historical information within these pages is based on fact and Cherokee legend, I must admit that references to "The Chosen Clan" and the "Sacred Forest" are my own creations.

Several books were used as reference material in the writing of this story, and I highly recommend them to anyone who is interested in learning more about the Cherokee people. They are: *Indians of North America, The Cherokee,* by Theda Perdue, Chelsea House Publishers. Alvin M. Josephy, Jr.'s *500 Nations (an Illustrated History of North American Indians)*, published by Alfred A. Knopf, New York, 1994. *Stories of The Yunwi Tsunsdi'*, (The Cherokee Little People), a Western Carolina University English 102 Class Project, edited by Jeannie Reed. *America's Fascinating Indian Heritage,* a 1978 *Reader's Digest* production.

There are many other informative Native American publications available, and I urge you to examine them through your local libraries.

As always, I am indebted to my wife, Chris, for her patience and ability in organizing my scribblings; and to her and my children, Camden and Daniel, for their support and understanding.

I wish to thank Mrs. Elizabeth Pickett and my aunt, Jeanne Clabough, for their editing skills and input on this project. They have helped to enhance a story which is very special to me. Thanks, also, to Judy Ligon for capturing the essence of **Wind Dancer's Flute**.

FEW
May 6, 1998

Francis Eugene Wood lives with his
wife and children in Sheppards, Virginia.

Titles by Francis Eugene Wood

The Wooden Bell (A Christmas Story)
The Legend of Chadega and The Weeping Tree
The Fodder Milo Stories
The Crystal Rose
The Angel Carver
The Nipkins

These books are available through the author's website at:
http://tipofthemoon.com
or
Write To:
Tip-of-the-Moon Publishing Co.
Route 2, Box 1725 • Farmville, VA 23901